WALT DISNEY PRODUCTIONS

presents

THUMPER

Random House  **New York**

First American Edition. Copyright © 1982 by Walt Disney Productions. All rights reserved under
International and Pan-American Copyright Conventions. Published in the United States by Random
House, Inc., New York, and simultaneously in Canada by Random House of Canada Limited, To-
ronto. Originally published in Denmark as STAMPE REDDER SINE VENNER by Gutenberghus
Gruppen, Copenhagen. ISBN: 0-394-85296-6 Manufactured in the United States of America
2 3 4 5 6 7 8 9 0 A B C D E F G H I J K

Book Club Edition

Deep in the middle of a forest lived
many animals.

Squirrels and birds made their home
in the forest.

Bambi, the young deer, lived there.

Flower, the skunk, lived there too.

They were very happy in their home.

A rabbit family also lived in
the forest.

Mother Rabbit had three children.
They kept her very busy.

There was Puffy, who
loved to play . . .

and Muffy, who
loved to eat . . .

and then there was
Thumper.

Every morning the rabbits went to
the meadow.

There they ate a breakfast of clover.

Then the little rabbits played.

Mother Rabbit watched her children
very carefully.
She told them to stay close to her.
She wanted them to be safe.

Every day Mother Rabbit taught her
children something new.

Puffy and Muffy were good little rabbits.
They sat and listened.
But Thumper always ran off.

One day Thumper went
to visit old Mr. Owl.
"Hello," said Thumper.
"Don't bother me now,"
said Mr. Owl. "I sleep
during the day."

"I'm sorry, Mr. Owl,"
said Thumper. "I will
come back another time."

Then Thumper ran to see his friend
Flower, the skunk.

The skunk children were playing near
a hollow log.
Thumper jumped up onto the log.
He thumped it loudly with his foot.

"That's wonderful," said Flower.
"How do you do that?"
    "It's easy," Thumper said.

Then Thumper
ran off to see
Bambi.

Thumper found Bambi
with his mother.
"May we play together?"
Thumper asked.

"Yes," said Bambi's mother.
"But don't go too far away."
"We won't," they said.

Soon Bambi and Thumper were running
through the tall grass.

Bambi and Thumper raced
into the forest.

Birds and frogs hurried
out of the way.

Bambi was faster than little Thumper.
"Be careful jumping over this log,"
said Bambi.
Too late!
Thumper tripped and fell.

But Thumper was not hurt.
He just laughed.
"It's a good thing you have
a fluffy tail to pad you,"
said Bambi.

Just then Bambi's mother called to him.
"Come back, Bambi. It's time to rest."
Thumper did not mind.

He saw his friend the butterfly and
went chasing after him.

"Where is Thumper?" said Mother
Rabbit. "I told him to stay nearby.
Now he is gone again."

"I don't see him," said Puffy.

"He will come back," said Muffy.

But Mother Rabbit was worried.

"I will go see Mr. Owl," she said.

Mr. Owl was angry when
Mother Rabbit woke him up.
"I'm sorry, Mr. Owl, but
Thumper is missing. Will
you try to find him?"

"Oh, all right,"
said Mr. Owl.
Off he flew.

Mr. Owl flew high and low, looking
for Thumper.
Suddenly he saw smoke and fire.
He flew back to Mother Rabbit.

"I did not see Thumper,"
said Mr. Owl. "But a fire
is coming! Run to the lake.
You will be safe there."

"I cannot leave without
Thumper," said Mother Rabbit.

"Don't worry," said
Mr. Owl. "I will find
him and bring him to
you."

And off he flew again.

"Hurry, children!" said
Mother Rabbit.
"But what about Thumper?"
asked Muffy.

"Mr. Owl will find him," said Mother Rabbit.
"And then Thumper will get a piece of my mind!"

Meanwhile Thumper was having fun
with his friend the butterfly.

He did not know there was a fire.

Mr. Owl spotted him from high above.

Mr. Owl flew down.
"Run, Thumper, run!
A fire is coming this
way!"

"Where is my family?" asked Thumper.

"They are safe by the lake," said
Mr. Owl. "Come, follow me."

"But I must warn
my friends," thought
Thumper.

So Thumper did not run
right to the lake.
He ran to find Flower
and her family.

He thumped loudly on a log.
The skunks came quickly.
"What is it, Thumper?" asked Flower.
"Fire! Fire!" shouted Thumper.
"Run for the lake!"

"You come too," said Mrs. Skunk.
"I will," said Thumper. "But first I
must warn Bambi and his mother."
"All right. But hurry," said Mrs. Skunk.
She scurried away with her family.

Thumper ran as fast
as he could.

He found Bambi and
his mother sleeping.

He thumped loudly
to wake them.

"What is it?" asked Bambi's mother.
"A fire is coming this way!"
said Thumper.

"We must run
to the lake!
Hurry!" said
Thumper.

The three of them ran as fast as they could.

But Thumper was slower than Bambi and his mother. Soon he was far behind.

A thunderstorm blew up.
CRACK! Lightning struck a tree.
The falling tree knocked Thumper
into a hole.

All the other animals were safe
at the lake.
The rain began to put out the fire.

"Thumper was wonderful," said Bambi.
"He saved our lives."

"But where IS Thumper?" asked Mother
Rabbit.

"I will look again," said Mr. Owl.

Finally Mr. Owl came back. "There is no sign of Thumper."

"I feel terrible," said Bambi. "We ran too fast. Thumper could not keep up."

"Thumper was very
brave to warn us,"
said Bambi's mother.
"He should have saved
himself."

But lucky Thumper was not hurt.
He had a bump on his head where
the falling tree hit him.
But he was safe in the big hole.
The fire did not touch him.

Drops of rain
woke Thumper up.

He crawled slowly
out of the hole.
The forest fire
was out.

He began to thump loudly on a hollow log.

Down at the lake, all the animals were sad.
They thought that they would never see
little Thumper again.

But suddenly they
heard something!

"That sounds like
Thumper!" cried
Mother Rabbit.

And it was!
A minute later Thumper
came running up.

Everyone was very happy to see Thumper.
"Hooray for Thumper!" they all shouted.
"He saved us from the terrible fire!"
"You are a hero, Thumper," said Muffy
and Puffy.

Mother Rabbit didn't say anything.
She just patted her son proudly.